Benny
Doesn't Like
to Be Hugged

Zetta Elliott

Benny
Doesn't Like
to Be Hugged

Illustrated by Purple Wong

Rosetta
Press

Books by Zetta Elliott

A Hand to Hold
A Wave Came Through Our Window
A Wish After Midnight
An Angel for Mariqua
Billie's Blues
Bird
Dayshaun's Gift
Fox & Crow: a Christmas Tale
I Love Snow!
Let the Faithful Come
Max Loves Muñecas!
Melena's Jubilee
Milo's Museum
Room In My Heart
Ship of Souls
The Boy in the Bubble
The Deep
The Door at the Crossroads
The Ghosts in the Castle
The Girl Who Swallowed the Sun
The Last Bunny in Brooklyn
The Magic Mirror
The Phoenix on Barkley Street

Benny likes trains that chug along the track.

Benny likes to eat seedless grapes for his snack.

Benny plays with quiet kids like Miko and Zach.

But Benny doesn't like to be hugged.

Benny likes cupcakes that aren't covered in sprinkles.

Benny likes clothes that don't have any wrinkles.

Benny can name the brightest star—
and he knows why it twinkles.

But Benny doesn't like to be hugged.

Sometimes Benny cries when the room gets too loud.

Sometimes he twirls away from the rest of the crowd.

When I tell a joke, Benny doesn't always smile.

And he can act fussy every once in a while.

But Benny's my best friend and I like him a lot.

If he needs things done a certain way,
I don't give it a second thought.

Because true friends accept each other just the way they are.

And being different is what makes us unique—
like a snowflake
or a star!

Author's Note

I am not autistic, nor am I an expert on ASD (autism spectrum disorder). I wrote this story because two of my friends have autistic sons and though I try to create inclusive books, I realized I didn't have any stories that represent neurodiversity. I have also marveled at the way my friends advocate tirelessly for their sons, both of whom are Black and so face additional challenges in a society set on disciplining Black boys. All children deserve a book that mirrors their reality, and I wanted to center an autistic Black boy in a story that celebrates difference.

I consider myself to be a highly sensitive person (HSP), and I've often wondered what it would be like to have experienced heightened sensitivity as a child. When I shared this story with a friend who has Asperger syndrome, she urged me to consider telling the story from Benny's point of view. Many fictional books about autistic children are told from the perspective of a family member or friend, and I'm afraid my book continues that trend. I was heartened, however, when Dorothy read the book and thanked me for giving Benny a friend. One book can't represent the range of experiences of children on the autism spectrum, but I hope Benny and his friend offer readers a model of compassion and understanding.

I would like to thank my friends Dorothy, Renae, and Lyn for sharing their experiences and expertise with me. Another friend, Debbie Reese (Nambe Pueblo), once pointed out that I didn't have any Native American children represented in my books. She suggested that I signify Indigenous identity by having a child wear an item of clothing with an identifiably Native logo. I asked my illustrator to reproduce Super Indian on one boy's t-shirt, and the comics' creator granted me permission after we were introduced by Debbie. I'm grateful that Debbie helped me remedy this omission, and I'd like to thank Arigon Starr (Kickapoo) for allowing me to include this small but empowering image of her superhero. You can read about the adventures of Super Indian at www.superindiancomics.com

This is my fifth collaboration with Purple Wong, an extremely talented illustrator based in Hong Kong. I would like to thank her for rendering Black children so beautifully, and for ensuring that our books reflect the diversity of the world in which we live.

~ Zetta Elliott
9/22/17

Resources

The Color of Autism
www.thecolorofautism.org

Autism in Black
www.autisminblack.com

Hatching Hope Foundation
www.hatchinghope.org

The Chaka Supports Autism Initiative
www.chakafoundation.org/chakasupports.php

HollyRod Foundation
www.hollyrod.org

Wrong Planet
www.wrongplanet.net

DragonBee Press
www.autisticgirls.com

ABOUT THE AUTHOR

Zetta Elliott is the award-winning author of over twenty-five books for young readers. She lives in Brooklyn and believes sensitivity is a strength.

Learn more at www.zettaelliott.com

ABOUT THE ILLUSTRATOR

Purple Wong is an illustrator and graphic designer based in Hong Kong. She works with a diverse range of international clients, creating illustrations for publishing, advertising, education, and more. She also draws inspiration from ordinary things, especially from nature.

Jump into her fantasy world at www.behance.net/purplewong

Rosetta Press

Rosetta Press publishes books for children with the following objectives:

1. To generate culturally relevant stories that center children who have been marginalized, misrepresented, and/or rendered invisible in children's literature.

2. To produce affordable, high-quality books so that families—regardless of income—can build home libraries that will enhance their children's academic success.

3. To produce a steady supply of compelling, diverse stories that will nourish the imagination and excite even reluctant readers.

All Rosetta Press titles are available online and can be ordered from major distributors by bookstores and libraries. E-books are available in the Kindle Store.

Made in the USA
Monee, IL
11 February 2021